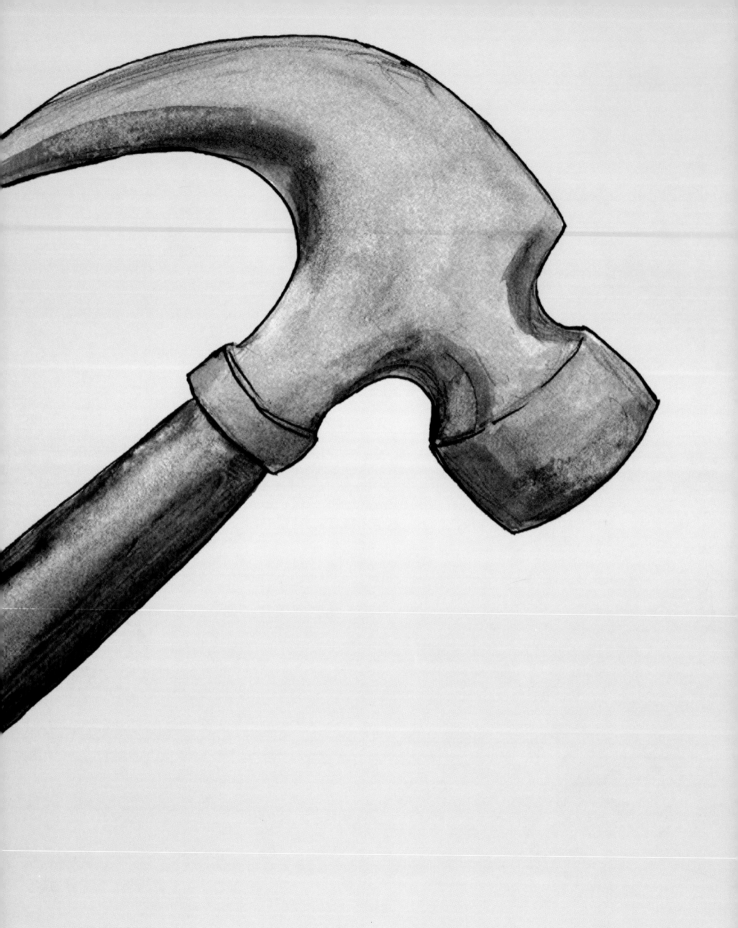

BANG
BANG
BANG
HAMMERS IN THE MORNING

WRITTEN AND ILLUSTRATED BY
BETTY FRITZ

Kinderhaus Publishing Company, Glendale CA
www.kinderhauspublishing.com
Printed in China
First Edition, 2009

CPSIA Tracking Label Information
Production Location: Guangdong, China
Production Date: 11-09-2009
Cohort: Batch 1

Library of Congress Control Number: 2009910182
ISBN 978-1-61623-624-3

The artwork for this book was prepared with watercolor paints.

Many thanks to my husband
who allowed me to be "GENERAL"
during our home renovation phase.

And to my 3 children
who inspired me to put our adventurous
experiences and memories into print.

Finally, a big heart-felt thanks to our friends and
family who either lent a hand, offered a shower,
gave advice, or simply just listened.

R-E-N-O-V-A-T-I-O-N
Renovation?

Mom and Dad say we are starting our house renovation next week.

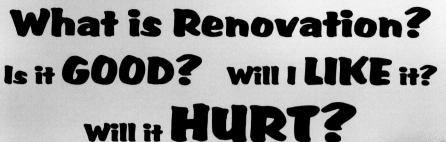

What is Renovation?
Is it GOOD? will I LIKE it?
will it HURT?

I guess I looked a little perplexed because Mom and Dad laughed and immediately assured me that renovation was a good thing. We simply rip down our house and build a better and newer one.

Wow...
COOL!!

I asked them where we would all go while this was happening and do you know what they said?

"NOWHERE.
We will just stay right HERE!!"

My Mom and Dad plus my baby
brother and I will all live in my
parent's bedroom until it is
all done.

It will be like camping
in our own house.

What an adventure!!

As the big start day approaches, I start packing up all my stuff to move into Mom and Dad's room. They've got a **BIG** room so there should be lots of space for everthing...
including...
my hamster,
and my rock collection,
and my big wheel,
and my really cool play car garage.

So...back and forth down the hall I go...
load after load...
carrying **ALL** my stuff
to their room.

Meanwhile, my Mom is packing up all my baby brother's stuff.
He is really small so he can't possibly need that much stuff.

But **WAIT**...
first I see his crib rolling down the hall...
then his changing table...
AND his big humongous box of diapers.
Mom and Dad's room is really filling up!!

It is not looking so big anymore.

Wait a second...
Where will MY bed go?
Do you know what they said?

"Oh no...you won't be bringing your bed in here.
It is **WAY** too big...
You will be sleeping on Dad's
old army cot at the
end of our bed."

WOW...
An army cot.
HOW COOL!!

Finally, the **BIG** day is tomorrow.
I can't wait!!

Tonight is the last day I will ever sleep in my **OLD** room.

**I am so excited.
I can hardly sleep.**

S	M	T	W	T	F	S
			1	2	3	4
5	6	7	8	9	10	11
12	13	14	15	16	17	18
19	20	21	22	23	24	25
26	27	28	29	30	31	

March

But Morning does come...
BANG BANG BANG
I groggily open an eye.

BANG BANG BANG

I shake my head.
What is that NOISE?
It is only SEVEN in
the morning!!

This is EARLY!!
I jump out of bed
and look for my
Mommy.

Mom is upstairs talking to this guy wearing a BIG YELLOW HARD HAT.

He sees me and smiles.
Then he reaches over to his bag and pulls out another hard hat and puts it right on top of my head.

He says he is the **BIG GENERAL**
...and I'll be **Li'l General.**

COOL!!
That works for me.

Mom quickly makes me some breakfast
and gets me ready for school.
I am really **MAD** because
I DO NOT WANT TO LEAVE!!
How can I be expected to concentrate at school while all
this excitement is going on at my **HOUSE?**
It is not **FAIR!!**

They might need the services of Li'l General.
Mom won't listen and takes me anyways.
The hours pass by really slowly but finally
the bell rings and it is time to go home.

YAY!!

As we drive up to the house, I don't notice anything too different. Quickly, I jump out of the car and race to the front door. Mom yells after me...

"BE CAREFUL!!"

I swing open the front door and gasp as I look straight through to the back yard. There is no more back wall...

Just the **BACKYARD.**

This is soooo **COOL!!**

The next day we lose our kitchen. Mom has to cook dinner on the **BARBEQUE**. She also has all these cooking pots and toasters with long electric cords which she plugs into a big electrical power strip.

It looks like a **COLOSSAL TANGLE** of cords criss-crossing **EVERYWHERE!!**

Toward the end of the week, the weather starts to get ugly. Dad scans the weather stations listening to the reports.

"Looks like we are in for some **BIG RAIN!!**"

Oh...that can't be so good. Plus, it really is starting to get **COLD!!**   Dad lights a fire in the fireplace.

We all huddle around the warm fire and I ask Mom if we can roast some marshmallows.

It was just like... **CAMPING!!**

The next day was kind of a **DRAG.**
Not only did the ladder get taken away but the water was
turned off. This was a real **PAIN.**

I couldn't get a drink of water.
I couldn't fill up my water guns.
I couldn't mix my paints
and I couldn't even flush the toilet.

But on the bright side...No water meant
....NO SHOWERS!!

Whoo hoo!!

Mom had to fill up **BUCKETS** of water from an outside faucet and then carry them back into the house.

She then boiled some of it so that she could wash my dirty face and dirty hands.

She even made me some yummy HOT COCOA.

Just like camping!!

THE END

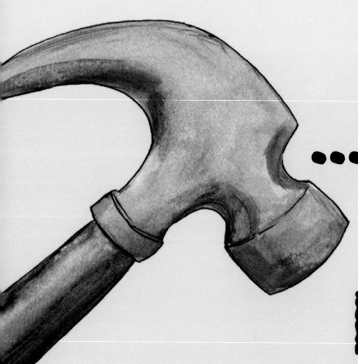

...or is it?

BANG
BANG
BANG